W9-CIE-937

Quentin Blake

ZAGAZOO

ORCHARD BOOKS
New York

For Tom

First American edition 1999 published by Orchard Books
First published in Great Britain in 1998 by Jonathan Cape

Orchard Books, A Grolier Company
95 Madison Avenue, New York, NY 10016

The text of this book is set in 24 point Monotype Horley Old Style.
The illustrations are watercolor. 10 9 8 7 6 5 4 3 2 1
Manufactured in Singapore

Library of Congress Cataloging-in-Publication Data
Blake, Quentin.
Zagazoo / by Quentin Blake.—1st American ed. p. cm.
Summary: The postman brings George and Bella a delightful pink creature, who suddenly turns into a vulture, a warthog, a dragon, a hairy monster, and other destructive and annoying creatures.
ISBN 0-531-30178-8 (trade : alk. paper)
[1. Animals—Fiction. 2. Monsters—Fiction.] I. Title.
PZ7.B56Zag 1998 [E]—dc21 98-42420

Once upon a time there was a happy couple.
Their names were George and Bella.

They spent their days

making model airplanes . . .

dusting . . .

and eating strawberry-and-vanilla ice cream.

One day the postman brought them a strange-looking parcel.

They unwrapped it together.

Inside, there was a little pink creature, as pretty as could be. On it was a label, which said:

Its name is ZAGAZOO.

How lovely it was! George and Bella spent happy days throwing it from one to the other.

Zagazoo was not *quite* perfect.

But his happy smile
seemed to make
up for that...

and George and Bella went
on happily throwing him to each other,
higher and higher.
It was a wonderful life.

AND THEN ONE DAY...

. . . George and Bella got up in the morning and discovered that Zagazoo had changed into a huge baby vulture.

Its screeches were terrifying.

They were even worse at night.

"What shall we do?" said George.
"How can we stand it?"

But then . . .

. . . they got up one morning and discovered that Zagazoo had changed into a small elephant.

He knocked over the furniture.

He pulled the tablecloth off the table.

He ate anything he could lay his trunk on.

"This is awful!" said Bella.
"How can we cope?"

But then . . .

. . . one morning they got up
and discovered that Zagazoo had
changed into a warthog.

He rolled about in anything that looked like mud and ran about the house with it.
"This is dreadful," said George.
"There's just no end to it."

But then . . .

. . . they got up one morning and discovered that Zagazoo had changed into a small, bad-tempered dragon.

He scorched the carpet.

He set fire to the sweater of a neighbor who had come to sell magazine subscriptions.

"This is terrible," said Bella. "In no time he's going to burn the house down."

But then . . .

. . . they got up one morning
and discovered that Zagazoo had
changed into a bat that hung
on to the curtains and wailed.

And then the next day he was the
warthog again.

And then some days he was the elephant . . .

and some days he was the bad-tempered dragon.

"This is driving us crazy!" said Bella. "If only he'd stay one thing."

But then . . .

. . . one morning they got up and Zagazoo had changed into a strange, hairy creature.

"Oh no!" said Bella. "I preferred the elephant."
"Or even the warthog," said George.

Every day the creature grew bigger... and hairier... and stranger.

"Suppose it never stops," said Bella.

"I can't bear to think about it," said George.
"It's turning my hair gray already.

What will become of us?"

BUT THEN. . .

. . . one morning George and Bella got up and discovered that Zagazoo had changed into a young man with perfect manners.

"Let me get you a chair, Mama," he said.

"And let me get you both some breakfast."

"And if there are any odd jobs that need doing, just let me know."

Zagazoo soon made friends with a young woman named Mirabelle.

They found they were both interested in motorcycle maintenance . . .

flower arrangement . . .

and eating fruit salad.

It was not long before
they knew that they wanted
to spend the rest of
their lives together.

But when they went to tell George
and Bella, they discovered that they had
changed into a pair of large brown pelicans.

You could tell they were pleased by the news
from the way they clattered their beaks.

Isn't life amazing!